Something Girl

Beth Goobie

Maria deMichele

orca soundings

ORCA BOOK PUBLISHERS

Library and Archives Canada Cataloguing in Publication

Goobie, Beth, 1959-
Something girl / Beth Goobie.

(Orca soundings)
ISBN 1-55143-347-8

I. Title. II. Series.

PS8563.O8326S64 2005   jC813'.54   C2005-900420-7

Summary: Will Sophie speak up about the abuse at home?

First published in the United States, 2005
Library of Congress Control Number: 2005920478

Orca Book Publishers gratefully acknowledges the support for its
publishing programs provided by the following agencies:
the Government of Canada through the Department of Canadian
Heritage's Book Publishing Industry Development Program (BPIDP),
the Canada Council for the Arts, and the British Columbia Arts Council.

Edited by: Melanie Jeffs
Cover design: Lynn O'Rourke
Cover photography: Firstlight.ca

Orca Book Publishers
PO Box 5626, Stn. B.
Victoria, BC Canada
V8R 6S4

Orca Book Publishers
PO Box 468
Custer, WA USA
98240-0468

08 07 06 • 5 4 3 2 1

Printed and bound in Canada.

for Otis, Nathan, Doug and Shane

Chapter One

My boyfriend, Larry, was driving me back from a dance at a high school across town. He pulled his car up to the curb outside my house. It was past my curfew, so I opened my door and started to get out.

"Hey," Larry shouted. As usual his stereo was on loud, the bass booming.

"What?" I shouted back, keeping my door open. I'd promised my dad I wouldn't be late. He was going to be mad about this, really mad.

Larry rolled his eyes and turned down the stereo. "Well, uh, Sophie," he said, tapping his fingers nervously on the steering wheel. Then he said, "I think I'll be going out with Wendy from now on. So it's over between us, okay? I'll still see you around school, and we can talk if you want, but that's all. Don't get your hopes up and try to get me to change my mind, because I won't."

I sat there, just staring at him. The fact that he was breaking up with me wasn't a surprise. Neither was Wendy—he'd spent all night dancing with her. It was just that I didn't know what to say. I never do. I'm completely dumb and boring—a waste of time to talk to.

Stupid, I thought, looking down at my feet. *Stupid, no good, nothing girl.*

"So," said Larry, revving the engine. "See you, I guess."

Then he turned the stereo back up, so I got out. Before I'd even closed the door, he took off down the street, tires squealing. For a moment I just stood there, staring after him. We'd been going out for three months, and every day I'd been expecting him to break up with me. I was surprised it had taken him so long, actually.

I started up the front walk to my house. As I did, the door opened and there was my dad. He didn't say anything, just stood and watched me. Right away I got a creepy feeling in my back—cold and tingly at the same time. Something was going to happen—I knew it was.

"Late again?" he said as I got close. "Get in here, now."

My knees went weak, and my heart started pounding through my whole body. I squeezed past him in the doorway, trying not to touch him, but he grabbed my arm. Then he closed the door and shut off the porch light.

There was no light inside the house. Everything was in shadows—just me and my dad and his big dark anger. Before I could move, he grabbed my head with both hands.

"Coming in late," he hissed. "Breaking your curfew. Waking me up in the middle of the night. And you're on probation for stealing. Hanging around with a no-good boyfriend who'll get you into more trouble. Trouble, trouble, trouble—you're nothing but trouble."

He banged the back of my head against the wall. "Stupid," he said. Then he banged it again. "No good," he said. He banged it again. "Nothing," he said.

Then he just kept banging my head against the wall. *Bang bang bang*. My brain was sliding around in waves of blackness. *Bang bang bang*. There was nothing I could do, nothing I could say. *Stupid, no good, nothing girl*.

Finally my dad stopped. He let go of my head and let me slide down the wall to the floor. For a moment we stayed like that. He leaned over me and panted. I sat there holding my head, just to make sure it was still there.

Then my dad turned and went upstairs. I listened to his footsteps walk up each stair, then into his bedroom. The bed squeaked as he got in and lay down. I could tell he'd left the door open. This meant I was going to have to be extra quiet going past it when I went to my room.

If I could stand up, that is. When I tried to lift my head, the pain was like a gun going off. It hurt to rest it against the wall, and it hurt to let it just hang. So I sat with my chin in my hands, trying to hold my head steady and away from the pain. This helped, but after a while my arms started to wobble.

I put my hand in my mouth and bit down on it hard, so it hurt more than my head. Then I made myself stand up and start climbing the stairs. The whole time I kept biting my hand so I wouldn't think about my head. When I got to the top of the stairs, I stopped and listened. I couldn't hear my dad snoring, so he had to be awake. Just thinking about this made my head hurt more, so I bit down harder on my hand and started down the hall.

Quiet, I was being quiet. I was tiptoeing. But when I got to my dad's door, he was standing in it and watching me.

"I'm sorry," I whispered, not looking at him. *Please, please*, I thought. *Don't hurt me. Just let me go to bed, please.*

He didn't say anything, just watched me go past him and down the hall. When he got like this—quiet and staring—it was the worst. Anything could happen—anything.

But tonight he just watched me. Quiet as anything, I walked past him and into my room. I didn't close my door because that would make him mad. I got straight into bed without undressing. Then I lay there in the dark, trying to listen past the pounding of my heart.

I couldn't hear anything. This meant he could still be standing in his doorway, listening. Or he could have gone back to bed. Or he could be right outside my door, waiting to see if I made any noise. Whatever I did now, I couldn't make any noise. It was important to be absolutely quiet. I couldn't roll over. I couldn't breathe heavily. I had to be quiet, *quiet*, QUIET.

I had to pee like crazy. I'd drunk two pops at the dance, which was stupid. *Stupid, no good, nothing girl*. I should have known better than to drink anything. Now I was going to have to hold it all night.

Was he out there listening?

Quiet, I had to be *quiet*.

Chapter Two

When I woke the next morning, my dad was gone for the day. I could tell by the way the house felt, as if there was more space in it. Even on Saturdays my dad went to his office, where he sold real estate. Like he said, he had to bring in the money to take care of my mom and me.

I was glad he was gone, so I could get up slowly. My head still hurt and my body felt heavy and slow, as if I was getting old. I went downstairs, step by step, really carefully. I tried not to think about what had happened last night. That was over and done with, and today was another day. Like my dad said, it was important to start each morning completely fresh.

My mom was sitting in the kitchen when I came in. She didn't look at me, just stared out the window. It was a nice day outside, but she stared out windows a lot. Too much. It was kind of hard to take sometimes.

"Your dad told me to tell you to mow the lawn," she said. "He wants it done before he gets home tonight, and no excuses."

I nodded. I had mowed the lawn last weekend and the grass had hardly grown. But my dad liked things to look good. A real estate agent's house had to look the best on the block.

After that my mom just stared out the window. I didn't tell her anything about my date with Larry and she didn't ask. I used to tell her things and she would ask questions. But now she just stared out the window, so it was like talking to no one.

I ate some cornflakes, then went outside and mowed the lawn. This made my head hurt worse, so I took some aspirin. Then I biked to the river to visit an old fort that my friend Jujube and I had built. It was made of old boards and a large piece of metal, nothing much. But some trees hid it, and no one knew about it but Jujube and me. This made it a good place to go when things got bad at home.

When I got to the river, I wheeled my bike into the trees and locked it. Then I lifted the blanket we'd hung over the fort's doorway and crawled inside. There were more blankets on the floor, and some old sofa pillows. It was a bit hot and smelled like old sofas. But when I lay down, I got really sleepy. It was different here from everywhere else, just lying in the fort with the river making pretty sounds close by. I didn't have to worry about my dad telling me to keep quiet. I didn't have to worry about not having my schoolwork done, or other kids laughing at me. I didn't even have to wonder why my mom stared out the window instead of talking to me. I could just breathe and look at the sun shining through the cracks between the boards. It was so nice, not having to worry.

I think I fell asleep, because suddenly I heard someone crawling into the fort. Right away fear slammed through me the way it does when I'm surprised. I thought, *It's my dad!* But then I saw it was Jujube and relaxed.

Jujube got her nickname from those bright jelly candies. One of her eyes was blue and the other green. It made her look kind of alien. When I first met her, I wanted to call her E.T. but there was a spaced-out kid down the street who already had that nickname.

I got to know Jujube because I used to babysit her. Now she was twelve and kind of young for me to be friends with, since I was fifteen. But she was smart, and I liked the way she was always talking. I wasn't a talker. I mostly just listened—like my mom, I guess.

"Froggy!" said Jujube, sitting down beside me.

Froggy was my nickname around the neighborhood. My dad gave it to me when I was little. I'm not sure why. Maybe he thought I looked like a frog or something.

"Yeah?" The aspirin I'd taken was wearing off. My head was starting to hurt again. I wasn't really in the mood for Jujube's talk.

She poked me in the arm and leaned close. "You won't believe it," she said with a grin. "I've figured out the next place the aliens are going to land."

I rolled my eyes. Aliens again. Jujube was always talking about them. So I just said, "You watch *The X-Files* too much."

"It's a good show," she said. Then she handed me a bag of salt-and-vinegar chips. "Here."

"Thanks." I tore open the bag and started

eating. As usual, I was starved. It was probably way past lunchtime.

"Where did you get that bruise?" asked Jujube.

"What bruise?" I stared at her. How could she see the bruises on the back of my head?

"There." She pointed to my arm. When I looked at it, I saw some purple fingermarks. *My dad!* I thought. *Last night*. But I shrugged as if it didn't matter.

"I bumped into something," I said.

Jujube sighed, and it got really quiet. Then she must have decided to change the subject because she said, "I've figured something out. Something really interesting."

Jujube was smart and liked to show off her brain. She won science awards and got a lot of ideas. I called them her "crazies," but I was kidding. She really was smart.

"The aliens visit Planet Earth every 3,594 months." Jujube talked slowly, as if she was announcing the discovery of a new planet.

"Uh-huh," I said, trying not to laugh. "What about it?"

Jujube's voice sped up so fast, I think it got ahead of her brain. "Well," she said, "aliens always leave a sign to show where they've been. I've seen it in pictures of their landing sites. You have to look really close, but it's there. It's awesome."

"What sign?" I asked.

"It looks like three triangles," said Jujube. She pulled a notebook and a pencil out of her pocket and drew a picture. It looked like three triangles that had bumped into each other.

"So?" I asked.

Jujube's mouth just kept going. "The first place they landed was in the Middle East," she said. "I think most aliens land there first. Maybe it's like a cosmic energy place, or something. Then it was South America, in the Andes. I think they're going to land here next."

This was too much, and I started to laugh.

"In Edmonton?" I said. "This is one of your crazies, right?"

Jujube sucked in her lips, then decided to ignore me. "The way I figure it," she said, "the aliens will show up in Edmonton about a month from now—summer vacation."

I wasn't looking forward to July. My dad would be home on vacation from his real estate office for a whole month.

"Do they take people with them?" I asked, half serious.

"Only one-way tickets," Jujube grinned.

I gave a long sigh. To be able to lift up and float away from all my problems…If only life was like that—aliens dropping by to rescue the nothing girl. If only.

Chapter Three

Jujube waited while I finished the bag of chips. Then we crawled out of the fort and headed over to her house. She wanted to show me something she'd found in her science books about aliens. It was more of her crazies, but I was still hungry and hoping for some lunch. I could listen to anything as long as I was eating.

I doubled Jujube on my bike, but we got off and walked when we got to her street. Her mom didn't like me giving Jujube rides on my bike. She said it wasn't safe. My mom never said anything about it. Too busy staring out windows, I guess.

When we got to Jujube's block, I pulled down my T-shirt sleeve to cover the bruise on my arm. If Jujube's mom saw it, there would be trouble. She always asked about the littlest things—bruises, a bump on my head, even why I looked tired. She noticed way too much.

"Did you tell your mom anything about that bump I had on my head?" I asked Jujube.

Jujube started staring at the ground, as if she thought aliens were going to crawl out of the grass. I tried to get a good look at her eyes. When Jujube was nervous, the green eye got greener.

The green eye looked very green.

"Jujube," I hissed. "You promised you wouldn't tell."

Jujube didn't look at me. Instead she took off, running down the sidewalk toward her house. This meant trouble—big trouble. My head started pounding like crazy.

"What did you tell her?" I shouted.

"Nothing," Jujube called back at me. "I didn't tell her anything."

"How come you won't look at me then?" I yelled. What if Jujube's mom noticed the new bruise on my arm? She would ask questions for sure. Then another social worker would come to my house. After he left, my dad would beat me up worse than last time. He told me it was my fault social workers kept showing up and making him look bad with the neighbors. And he said it was my job to make sure no one asked any more questions.

I dropped my bike and took off after Jujube. When I caught up to her, I grabbed her arm.

Jujube tried to pull away. "She kept asking, Froggy," she said. "That was an awesome bump you had."

"You didn't have to tell her!" I shook her a little. My heart was pounding so hard I could barely think.

"I didn't tell her that much." Jujube started to cry. This made me feel bad, so I dropped her arm. "I told her you fell, just like you wanted me to," she said.

I wasn't sure I believed her, but I let it go. What could I do? I would just have to be extra careful and make sure I covered the bruise on my arm. And I would have to make sure no one could tell how bad my head hurt. It sure was pounding. With a groan, I locked my bike to a street sign and followed Jujube into her front yard.

Just then Jujube's neighbor, Rick, came around the side of his house. He was sixteen and in the drama club at my high school, Scona High. Lots of girls liked him.

"Hi, Jujube," he called. "Hi, Sophie."

I could feel myself going red, so I stared at the ground. Jujube waved back and called, "Hi, Rick." She was in her first year at McKernan Junior High, and she wasn't into guys yet. She was into aliens.

"Hey, Sophie, you going to the end-of-the-year school dance?" Rick started walking toward us.

"Maybe." I kept looking at the ground. I was getting redder—I could feel it. I hated it when I did that. Most girls didn't go radioactive just because a guy talked to them. Why couldn't I be normal? *Stupid, no good, nothing girl.*

Rick stopped on the other side of the fence and smiled at me. All I could do was stare at my feet. I wished he would go away. If he stuck around, he would find out how dumb and stupid I was—just like Larry had. Thinking about this made my head pound even harder.

"Maybe I'll see you there," Rick said.

"Maybe." I tried to think of something else to say, but my head hurt too much. Fortunately, Jujube started going into her house. As I turned to follow, my right foot stepped on my left and I almost tripped. *Stupid, no good, nothing girl.* My dad was right—I couldn't even walk properly.

As soon as we got inside, Jujube went into the kitchen and took out some bread, peanut butter and jam. Then she went off to find her spaced-out science books, while I sat at the table making sandwiches. When she came back, my mouth was full of peanut butter. I was halfway through my second sandwich.

Jujube opened her books and started pointing at pictures. "Here they are—the triangles. They're on the side of this hill. Can you see them?"

I couldn't see any triangles, but maybe the peanut butter had glued my brain shut. "Nope," I said.

Jujube frowned and flipped to another page. "How about here—can you see the triangles in the pyramids?"

"But the pyramids are triangles," I said. I didn't think that proved anything, but Jujube looked happy.

"Now look here," she said, "in this picture of these old rocks. There are triangles in them, see?"

There were some weird lines in the rocks, but I thought they might be from snakes or fossils. I was about to tell Jujube this, but then her mom walked into the room. Right away some peanut butter got stuck in my throat.

"Hello, Froggy," she smiled.

I grabbed one of Jujube's books and started staring at it. Jujube's mom sat down beside me. "How's your head?" she asked.

I nodded and kept staring at the book. Maybe she would think I was reading it. I turned a page and tried to look interested.

Jujube's mom sighed. "Jujube said you fell," she said.

Jujube poked me and grinned. "She's all better now, Mom," she said.

Jujube's mom's eyes are both green. They can zero in on you like two lasers. "Did you really fall, Froggy?" she asked.

I stared at Jujube's book. If only it could tell me something about how to make my dad love me. Or how I could make myself good enough so he *could* love me.

No questions, that was what he'd said. "Yeah," I told Jujube's mom. "I fell."

"Does Rose know about your head?" she asked.

Rose was my mom. When Jujube's mom said that, I knew I had to get out of there. She was definitely asking too many questions, and it was my job to make sure she didn't. But as I stood up, Jujube's mom grabbed my hand and held it. Quick as anything, I covered the bruise on my arm with my other hand.

Jujube's mom didn't notice. Instead she said, "Froggy, if you ever want to talk about anything, remember that I'm here. I'll listen to whatever you want to talk about."

I looked at her face. She was worried about me, I could tell. But what could she do? If I told her about my dad, she would try to talk to him. And he would kill me after she went home. Besides, I was the real problem in my family, not my dad. I was the one he couldn't love. No one would ever be able to love someone like me—*stupid, no good, nothing girl*.

"Let's go," I said to Jujube and pulled my hand out of her mom's. We went outside and I unlocked my bike. Rick had gone inside, so no one else was around.

"Jujube," I said, "you *have* to listen to me." I knew I had to get her to understand so she wouldn't blab anymore to her mom. So I talked slowly and quietly, but like I meant it. "If your mom finds out how I got that bump on my head and the bruises and stuff, she'll tell a social worker," I said. "If a social worker comes to my house, my dad will really come after me. I can't stop him, Jujube. I'll get hurt bad."

Jujube just stared at me, her face blank. She wasn't getting it.

I tried to scare her some more, to *make* her not tell. "They'll send me to a group home," I said, "away from my own house and my mom and dad. Weirdos and freaks live in group homes. I'm not a weirdo and I don't want to live in a group home. Not now and not ever. Do you get it?"

Then I got onto my bike and took off out of there.

Chapter Four

It was Monday morning, 8:50 AM. "O Canada" had just finished blasting out of the PA, and my homeroom class finally got to sit down. Then someone came on the PA and talked about the end-of-the-year dance. It made me think about Larry, and I felt kind of sick. I wasn't looking forward to bumping into him in the halls.

"Could I talk to you for a minute, Sophie?" It was my homeroom teacher, Mr. Taylor. A lot of kids liked him because he really paid attention to what you said. But I thought it was too much attention. He was like Jujube's mom, noticing the littlest things.

I walked up to his desk and tried to smile. "Good morning, Mr. Taylor. How are you?"

"I'm fine, Sophie," he said, smiling back at me. "And how are you? How was your weekend?"

I knew it—more questions. My heart started to pound so hard it hurt. I wasn't supposed to let questions happen. My dad had said no questions—that was my job.

"I'm fine, Mr. Taylor," I said, looking at my feet. "Everything's awesome."

"That's quite a dark bruise you've got on your arm," he said.

Quickly I looked at my arm. When I'd put on my T-shirt this morning, the sleeves had covered the bruise. But by the time I'd gotten to school, the bottom of the sleeves had ridden up. Now you could see the bruise, and it was even darker than it had been on Saturday. There were my dad's fingermarks, clear as anything.

Before I could answer, Mr. Taylor said, "Are you sure everything is fine, Sophie? You also had that bump on your forehead a few weeks ago."

I started counting inside my head, really slowly. It was a trick I used to slow down my thoughts when I got worried. Sometimes it helped me think straight.

"Skateboarding, Mr. Taylor," I said. Inside my head the numbers kept counting, slow and quiet. Now I could look straight at Mr. Taylor, almost in the eye. My voice wasn't even wobbly. My dad would have been proud of me, really proud. "I went off the curb and did a major flip-out," I said, as if it had actually happened.

Mr. Taylor looked at me for what felt like forever. I tried to keep looking back, but it was hard. He looked as if he really wanted me to talk to him, but how would that help?

If I talked to him, he would phone a social worker. The social worker would come to our house and talk to my dad. And after the social worker left, my dad would kill me.

For a second, just a second, I wondered what it would be like if Mr. Taylor was my dad. But then I realized it would probably be just the same. All dads hit their kids, didn't they? Every kid needed it sometimes, when something went wrong in their head. And I needed it more than most kids. Things were always going wrong in my head. If I could just figure out how to straighten out my head, things would be fine.

"I'm working hard and getting my home-work done," I told Mr. Taylor. "And I haven't been late for school in a couple of weeks."

"Yes." Mr. Taylor sounded tired. "Yes, that's true, Sophie."

The bell rang and kids started getting out of their desks.

"Can I go now?" I asked. "I don't want to be late for math."

"Okay, Sophie, you can go." Mr. Taylor leaned back in his chair and watched me go. I tried to walk slowly so I didn't look nervous. But once I was through the door, I took off. That had been close, really close. I was sure Mr. Taylor was about to send me to the counseling office.

When I got to my math class, I stood in the hall and tried to calm down. Nervous shakes were running through my whole body. *No questions*, I kept thinking. *I can't let any more questions happen.*

Slowly the shakes stopped and I looked up. That was when I saw Larry coming down the hall with Wendy. They were holding hands and laughing. Wendy pointed at me and said, "Hey, Larry, there's your ex." Larry looked at me and grinned.

I just turned and went into my math class. My heart was pounding, and I think I bumped into the doorframe. But I didn't start crying. I didn't let anyone see how much it hurt. Instead I kept thinking, *Don't let things get to*

you. You've got to be tough, got to be tough.
My dad said this a lot. He would have been
proud of the way I walked away from Larry,
really proud.

But when I sat down, I didn't feel so tough.
I couldn't get Larry out of my head. If only I
could be smart and funny and pretty so guys
would like me. If only I could giggle and say
the kinds of things they liked to hear, like
Wendy did. In all the time Larry and I had
gone out, he'd never held my hand. We'd
kissed sometimes when we were by ourselves
and no one could see us. But Larry had never
ever held my hand.

I spent the rest of the day trying not to
run into Larry again. After school I had a
math detention because I hadn't done my
homework. When I went out to the bike rack,
I saw Jujube sitting by my bike. She must
have called my house, then come looking for
me at Scona High.

"Hey, Froggy," she called.

I looked around, but it was so late most

kids had gone home. I was relieved—the last thing I needed was for someone at school to learn my nickname.

"C'mon," I said. "I'm late for an appointment with my probation officer."

"I wanted to tell you," Jujube said, getting to her feet. "I hooked up my bedroom lamp so I can shine it out my window. I'm reading a book about the Morse code and I'm testing it out with my lamp."

"Let me guess," I groaned as I unlocked my bike. "You're sending messages to aliens."

"They're more advanced than us," said Jujube, getting on behind me. "So they should understand the Morse code."

"Yeah," I said, starting off on my bike. "But will they understand *you*? That's the real question."

"Froggy!" said Jujube, holding tight as I went around a corner. "This is serious. I'm sending out important messages."

Suddenly I knew what she meant. She was sending messages about me into outer space.

They probably went something like this: *I've got a loser friend. She's cracking up. Her life's a mess and she won't go live in a group home. But she loves aliens. Come rescue her. Rescue the stupid, no good, nothing girl.*

Yeah right, I thought. *Me and the aliens in a cosmic group home. That'll be the day.*

I turned onto 82nd Avenue and biked slowly down the sidewalk. When I got to my probation officer's building, Jujube got off my bike and I locked it. As usual, I was late and kind of hungry. And also as usual, there was the sign, just waiting for me:

SOLICITOR GENERAL
CORRECTIONAL SERVICES
YOUNG OFFENDERS PROBATION

KNOCK LOUDLY IF YOU HAVE
AN APPOINTMENT

Chapter Five

I opened the door and walked into the office with Jujube behind me. Right away the secretary looked up from her desk and said, "You're late again, Sophie."

"I'm sorry," I said. "I had to stay after school to do some math."

The secretary frowned. "Didn't you tell them you had a meeting with your probation officer?"

I looked at my feet. Sometimes adults were really clued out. How was I supposed to tell my teacher I had a meeting with my probation officer in front of the whole class? The other kids already thought I was a loser.

But if the secretary didn't already understand this, she never would. So I didn't explain it to her. "Yeah," I lied. "My teacher made me stay anyway."

The secretary sighed. "Go on in," she said. "Ms. Lee is waiting for you."

I walked down a short hall to where Ms. Lee's office was. As I knocked on the door, I could hear Jujube talking to the secretary about aliens.

"Come in," said a voice.

I opened the door and saw Ms. Lee sitting behind her desk. "Sophie," she smiled. "Sit down and tell me how you are."

I sat down and tried to smile back at her. *Act cool*, I told myself. *It'll be okay if you don't tell her anything.*

Then I thought, *Is my bruise showing?* I looked at my arm and saw half the bruise sticking out from under the bottom of my sleeve. Quickly I pulled the sleeve down.

One, two, three, four, I thought, counting slowly in my head.

The questions started. I was on probation because I stole a few things from a store—lipstick, some chocolate bars and cigarettes. The cops caught me a couple of times, but I never had a whole bunch of stuff. I wasn't a crime wave. The time I took the chocolate bars, I was hungry. The cigarettes were a fluke, just sitting on the counter while a guy paid for them. And the time I took the lipstick, I was mad.

I didn't even wear lipstick. I knew it was dumb to steal, but some days I couldn't make myself care much.

"You skipped some classes last week," said Ms. Lee.

"Yeah," I said. It was hard to smile, listen and keep counting in my head. *Nine, ten, eleven*, I thought. "I'm sorry," I said. "I'll try harder."

"And you need to work harder on your schoolwork," said Ms. Lee.

"Yeah." *Fifteen, sixteen, seventeen, eighteen.* Every time I came here, we went through the same list of questions and answers. Why did we have to go through this crap?

"How are things at home?" asked Ms. Lee.

"Fine," I said.

"How are things with your dad?" Ms. Lee was watching me like a hawk.

"Fine." I kept counting in my head. *Twenty-five, twenty-six, twenty-seven.*

"How are things with your mom?" Ms. Lee asked.

"Fine," I said.

Ms. Lee sighed. "Who are you spending time with?"

Finally, an easy question. "Nobody much," I said. "Just Jujube."

"Sophie," Ms. Lee said softly. "Why do you have your hand over your arm?"

I looked at my arm. My hand was hanging onto the bottom of my sleeve, pulling it down over the bruise. *Thirty*, I counted in my head. *Thirty-one, thirty-two, thirty-three*. My heart was pounding so hard I could barely think.

Ms. Lee leaned forward. "Why don't you want me to see your arm, Sophie?"

"There's nothing wrong with my arm," I said. "Why are you making such a big deal out of it?"

"I'm not making a big deal out of it," she said, getting up. "I just want to see it." She came around the desk and put a hand on my shoulder. "C'mon, let me see."

"Skateboarding," I said quickly. "I was skateboarding with Jujube." But Ms. Lee just kept looking at me, so I had to take my hand off my arm. Slowly she lifted the bottom of my sleeve. The bruise was almost black, and it didn't look anything like a falling-down bruise. It looked like a grab bruise for sure.

"That's a pretty bad bruise," Ms. Lee said. "How did you really get it, Sophie?"

Forty-one, forty-two, forty-three. "Skateboarding with Jujube," I said, trying to sound as if I meant it. They couldn't do anything to my dad if I didn't tell the truth. If I just kept lying, they would have no proof.

Ms. Lee looked at me closely. "And that's how you got the bump on your forehead too?"

"I'm not very good at skateboarding," I said. I tried to look her straight in the eye. Did she believe me? *Did* she?

Ms. Lee took a step back. Then she said, "Did your father do this, Sophie?"

My heart just about exploded. "No!" I said. I stood up and took a step toward her. "My dad's a good dad," I said loudly. "He does his best for me and never hurts me. Never, not ever. Look, I promise I'll go to school every single day from now on. I won't steal anymore. I'll do whatever you say, okay? Is that okay?"

Ms. Lee went back to her desk and sat down. She looked at me quietly. "You're a really nice kid, Sophie," she said. "I want you to live in a place that's safe."

"I'm fine," I said. I was almost crying. I mean I was just *begging* her to believe me.

"No, you're not fine," Ms. Lee said. Then she opened her datebook and said, "I want to see you next week."

My heart stopped dead. Next week was extra. I was only supposed to see her every two weeks. "How come?" I asked slowly.

Ms. Lee handed me a card with a date and time written on it. "I want to make sure all this skateboarding doesn't break your leg," she said. "Next week, Monday at 4:00, like today."

"Okay," I said. What was I supposed to say—no?

I took the card and left, just glad to be out of there. One more question and she would have gotten it all out of me. As I walked into the waiting room, Jujube jumped up from her chair. Her green eye was very green, and she was holding something between her fingers.

"Look, Froggy," she said.

"What?" I asked, heading for the door. I was trying to figure out how I was going to tell my dad I had an extra meeting with Ms. Lee.

Jujube stuck a jawbreaker she'd been sucking into my face. It was slimy.

"Gross," I said and pushed it away.

"I sucked down to the red layer," she said, really excited. "I usually check all the layers to see what they look like. This time, on the red layer, three triangles showed up. Can you see it?"

I looked at the jawbreaker, but all I could see were wavy lines. Jujube was really losing it with this alien stuff. I sure knew how to pick my friends—she was crazier than I was!

But Jujube didn't think she was crazy. "In the Morse code I sent out last night," she grinned, "I asked them for a sign. I asked them for a sign *today*. And here it is!"

Chapter Six

I couldn't believe Jujube thought aliens had sent her a sign on her jawbreaker. But she kept going on and on about it, even when we went outside. I unlocked my bike, and she got on behind me. Then I took off, pedaling down 105 A Street. Jujube held out her jawbreaker, letting it dry in the wind. After a few blocks she put it into her pocket. I guess she wanted to keep it as proof of her contact with aliens.

Something was really going wrong with her brain, but I couldn't worry about it. I had enough to think about.

We headed over to her place. When we got there, Rick was sitting on his front porch. "Hi, Sophie," he called. "Hi, Jujube."

I concentrated on locking my bike to a street sign and trying not to turn red. When I looked up, Jujube had walked over to Rick and was sitting down beside him. I looked at the two of them, just sitting there like that. Jujube looked so relaxed, not even wondering whether Rick wanted her there or not. I always wondered if people were about to tell me to get lost.

I didn't sit down beside them. Instead I stood nearby, trying to look normal—not like I'd just come from an appointment with my probation officer.

"Hey, Rick," said Jujube. "D'you know anyone who lives in a group home?"

My heart stopped when she said that. For a second I thought Jujube and Rick had planned this conversation ahead of time. They were trying to get me to change my mind so I would want to move into a group home. That was it—Jujube had finally gotten tired of me. She wanted me to move into a group home so she wouldn't have to hang around with me anymore. So she'd asked Rick to help her convince me.

But Rick didn't look as if he was thinking about me at all. "Yeah," he said. "My friend Bert lives in one. He says it's not too bad. There are a lot of rules, but at least no one's taking it out on him just for breathing. And the staff are there to talk to if he wants."

"Why did he end up there?" asked Jujube.

"His parents kicked him around a lot," said Rick. "He used to blame himself for it—as if he made them do it. Crazy to think that way, but I guess it happens. He got his head on straight when he moved into the group home and talked things out with the staff."

I could tell Jujube was thinking hard. "Well, what's it like there?" she asked. "What do they feed him and stuff?"

Rick laughed. "Bread and water, Jujube." Then he shrugged. "Normal food, I guess. Just like anywhere else."

All of a sudden I had to get out of there. Maybe this was just a normal conversation. Maybe Jujube and Rick weren't trying to get me to move into a group home. Still, I knew my dad wouldn't want me listening to something like this. He wouldn't want me even *thinking* about group homes. Because if I moved into a group home, he would get into trouble. And I couldn't get my dad into trouble. He didn't deserve that.

"I've got to go," I said to Jujube. I started walking to my bike, and she came running after me. Neither of us said goodbye to Rick.

"Can't you stay for supper, Froggy?" Jujube said. "I asked Mom this morning and she said it was okay."

"No," I said and got onto my bike. "My mom told me to be home for 5:30."

But Jujube wouldn't let me go. She ran beside my bike, talking about aliens. More of her crazies. Suddenly it was too much and I blew up.

"Come on, Jujube," I snapped, stopping my bike. "Get real. There aren't any aliens except in the outer space inside your head."

Jujube looked as if I'd slapped her. Then she snapped back, "You're always mad at me. It's not my fault your life is so bad. It's your dad's. But you just let it happen. Why don't you want it to stop? Why don't you tell someone?"

I almost screamed at her, this made me so mad. How could she say something like that? How could she even *think* I wanted to get beat up? I was trying hard to change so my dad could love me. I just couldn't figure out what he wanted me to be.

I took off on my bike really fast, but Jujube's words kept running through my head. *You just let it happen. Why don't you want it to stop? Why don't you tell someone?* When I got home, I put my bike into the garage. Then I sat on the back porch and tried to calm down before I went in. My mom didn't notice when I was upset, but my dad did. If he noticed I was upset, he would ask questions. That was the last thing I needed.

So I made myself calm down, then went into the kitchen. My mom was sitting at the table, smoking. An empty beer bottle sat beside her hand—her usual afternoon drink. She looked okay, not like there had been any trouble. Sometimes my dad had to straighten out her head too. He would kick and hit her, but she was better than me at hiding the bruises. When I saw she was okay, I was so relieved I gave her a hug. She patted my arm.

"Hi, Froggy," she said. "You all right?"

"Yeah," I said. Then I waited to see if she would ask about my appointment with my probation officer. She didn't. She'd probably forgotten that I had one.

"I made you some hamburgers for supper," she said. "They're on the stove."

"Okay." I put a hamburger on a plate and brought it to the table. I tried not to look disappointed. We'd had hamburgers for supper three times the week before. But I guess my mom had more important things to worry about than making fancy suppers.

"Remember to keep your voice down," my mom said. "Your dad's talking to a client in the living room."

"Okay." I started to eat my hamburger, but then the kitchen phone rang. I got it after the first ring so it wouldn't disturb my dad's meeting.

"Hello?" I said in a low voice.

It was Jujube. "Froggy," she said. She sounded upset. "I'm sorry I said those things to you. Are you still mad at me?"

"No." Suddenly I felt mean for getting mad at her and taking off. She was worried about me; I knew that. She wasn't crazy. She was worried.

"Are you all right? Is everything all right?" Sometimes Jujube worried so much her voice squeaked.

"Yeah," I said. "I'm fine. But I've got to eat supper now. I'll call you later, okay?"

I could tell Jujube didn't want to hang up. But I couldn't spend my life on the phone just so she would know I was still kicking. I sat down beside my mom and started eating again. Then my mom stood up.

"I'm going to Bingo, hon," she said. "I left a note for your dad. I'll see you later, okay?"

She picked up her purse and went out the back door. After she left, I just sat there. I was still hungry, but I didn't feel like eating anymore. I guess I wanted my mom to sit with me while I ate supper—even if she stared out the window. It wasn't fun eating hamburgers by myself. So I just sat there like my mom and stared out the window.

Chapter Seven

As I stared out the window, I started to think. I remembered how my dad was nice to me and my mom sometimes. He wouldn't yell or hit. We would go on a holiday and get along the whole time. For a while we would seem like different people, a normal happy family. In a way this was worse, because I never knew when he would start up again. I always had to be on guard to see when he started to change. I had to be extra careful about what I said and did, so I didn't set him off. I never sat near him, even when he seemed all right. The farther away I was, the more time it gave me to run in case I said the wrong thing.

I heard my dad's client say goodbye in the hall. It sounded like Mr. Grant, one of our neighbors, so I poked my head through the doorway. My dad looked at me and smiled.

"Hello there, Froggy," said Mr. Grant. "How's school?"

"Okay," I said. "Everything's good."

"Glad to hear that," said Mr. Grant. "Well, thanks for everything, Tom. You've been a great help. I'll have to think about this some more." He shook my dad's hand.

Everyone looked up to my dad—he was good at his job and he was on a lot of committees. He even coached a boy's hockey team. I went to most of the games because I loved watching my dad while he was coaching. He was always calling out to the kids on the ice, telling them how to play better. They all liked him. I tried to learn hockey, but I wasn't very good.

Mr. Grant left and my dad closed the door behind him. Then he just stood for a moment with his back to me. Right away I started backing into the kitchen. My dad was being too quiet. If things were okay, he would be humming or whistling and moving around. When he finally turned around, his face had changed. No more smiling. It looked like a dead man's face.

"Stuffing your face again?" he asked.

I looked at my feet and tried to figure out how to get out of there without setting him off. "Just hamburgers," I said.

"Don't like the food here?" my dad said softly. "Going to complain to your probation officer?"

When he got mad, my dad's eyes looked black. They had no color and seemed to go on forever.

"I never complain to Ms. Lee," I said. "I only tell her good things."

A big weight was coming down on me—fear and more fear, and the feeling that it was going to happen again. It was going to happen and I couldn't stop it. No matter what Jujube and Ms. Lee and Mr. Taylor said, no one could stop this.

But I tried once more to get my dad to think about happy things. "How was your meeting?" I asked.

"Fine," he snapped. "Until the goddam phone rang. I almost had that sucker landed, and then the phone threw us off. It would've been an easy ten thousand bucks. But now he has to *think* about it some more. I'll bet it was your fault the phone rang, wasn't it, Froggy? It was one of your goddam friends."

When I heard my dad say "goddam," I turned into a black tornado inside, going round and round. Because when my dad swore, it was going to happen. There was no stopping it.

He yelled, "You think you own this house! You spend all your time on the phone. Your mother has to work part-time so we can feed you. You don't even go to school half the time."

He looked huge and dark, like in nightmares. I couldn't swallow. I couldn't talk. When I got scared like this, a hand came up from inside and grabbed all the words out of my mouth. My dad started coming toward me and everything went into slow motion. I tried to run into the kitchen, but every step seemed to take five minutes. So I grabbed a chair and pulled it in front of me. My dad picked it up and threw it across the room. Then he grabbed my arm.

"Stupid," he hissed. "No good. Nothing."

He started punching me, and I tried to cover myself with my other arm. But my dad pushed my face into the wall so I couldn't see what was coming next. Then he started kicking my legs and back. I felt like my gut was coming right out of me, as if I was turning into mush. I tried to pull free, but I couldn't. All I could think about was getting away away away.

Suddenly, inside my head, I saw the fort Jujube and I had built. I saw myself crawling inside the fort and trying to hide. I saw Jujube coming to find me and talking about aliens. "Aliens, aliens, aliens," I heard her say, over and over in my head.

Finally my dad stopped. He stood over me for a minute, breathing heavily. Then he turned and walked away. I heard him go upstairs, then back down again and out the front door. I don't know why he stopped when he did. Maybe he just got tired.

I was lying on the floor, next to the wall. It took a while to start moving. I wanted to get out of there in case my dad came back, but my legs wouldn't move. Each time I tried, a bright pain shot up my back. It was so bad I almost screamed, and once my head went black for a second. But after a while I just made myself. I got to my knees. Then I stood up. Then I walked to the downstairs bathroom and took a bunch of aspirin—around ten, I think. When I checked in the mirror, my face looked okay. My dad hardly ever hit me where people could see it.

The painkillers helped, but I still had to move slowly. I walked out the back door, carefully, like an old lady. Then I got out my bike. Getting onto it was hard, but then I could coast. I used back alleys so I didn't have to ride over curbs. When I got to the fort, I wheeled the bike into the trees and left it. I didn't lock it. I wasn't sure I could stand up that long.

I crawled into the fort and covered myself with a blanket. Then I lay there and tried not to moan. The pain was so big, it felt like it was everywhere. So I thought of a game I played when I was small. The game went like this—when my dad hit me, I would think of the pain as heat instead of hurt. Then I tried thinking of the pain as a nice heat, like a fireplace. I really had to think hard while I was getting hit, but I could usually make it work. Once I even laughed while my dad was hitting me, because it didn't hurt. I only did that once, because then he hit extra hard.

But tonight the game didn't work. The aspirin I had taken was wearing off, and the pain was getting bigger. Through the fort's door, I could see stars coming out, shining like far-off spaceships. But they were just stars. There weren't any aliens coming to save me from this pain.

Jujube's voice started up again in my head. *You just let it happen*, she said. *Why don't you want it to stop? Why don't you tell someone?*

What's to tell? I thought. *I don't want people to know my secret. I'm so dumb my dad has to hit me. Stupid, no good, nothing girl.*

My back was hurting so much I had to lie with my knees up in the air. It had never been this bad before, and I was scared like crazy. I was beginning to think I could never make my dad love me. Sometime he might really kill me, like in the stories I heard on the news. I couldn't figure out what to do, so I started to cry. The tears kept running down my neck and into my ears, but I couldn't turn my head because it hurt too much.

I think I passed out for a while because the next thing I knew, Jujube was there. She was sitting beside me in the dark, humming softly so she wouldn't wake me up.

Chapter Eight

Moonlight was shining through the door of the fort. It lit Jujube around the edges so she looked like an alien.

"You all right?" she asked.

It felt as if the pain in my back and legs had gone to sleep. I couldn't feel anything except a dull ache in my back. Still, I had a funny feeling something was wrong. I lay very still, trying to figure out what it was.

"What time is it?" I asked.

"Pretty late," said Jujube. "After ten, I think. Mom's working the nightshift. I called your house earlier—your dad said you were out."

Right away, I got worried. When Jujube's mom worked the nightshift, a neighbor lady slept over at their house. If she noticed Jujube was gone, there would be trouble.

"Jujube," I said, "there's no point in both of us flunking school. Why don't you go home and go to sleep?"

"I want to know how you are," she said.

I couldn't see her face, but I knew that tone of voice. When Jujube talked like this, there was no point in doing anything except what she wanted. So I tried to sit up, but a pain shot up my back as if two hands were tearing it apart. I fell back and held my breath, hoping the pain would go away. Then I heard loud groans and realized they were coming from me.

"Froggy?" Jujube's voice went up into a high squeak.

I didn't say anything. With all that pain in me, I was just thinking hard, trying to make it go away. When my back stopped hurting, I would figure out what to do next.

"I'm going to get Rick," Jujube said.

"No!" I shouted, but she was already gone. I could hear her footsteps running away, and then there was only the sound of the river out there in the night. It was swishing around, slow and steady—kind of like the pain in my back.

Then, somewhere off in the night, I heard a whine start up. At first I thought it was a mosquito, but it got closer and closer, louder and louder. Finally I figured out what it was. I tried to get up, but the pain shot through my back again and I couldn't move. When the ambulance pulled up outside the fort, its siren was the loudest thing I'd ever heard. Through the doorway, I could see flashing red lights. Then the siren shut off.

I heard Jujube say, "She's over here." Footsteps started coming through the trees.

"In here," said Jujube. Suddenly someone lifted the metal sheet that made up one side of the fort. The inside of the fort filled with red flashing lights. A woman leaned over me. She smelled like soap, the kind my mom used.

"You all right, kid?" she asked.

I wanted to say yes. I wanted to get up and walk away. All I could think of was how much trouble this was going to cause. There was no way I could hide the problem this time. My dad was going to get it big-time, and it was all my fault.

"No," I said. "My back hurts."

"Let me check it," said the woman. "Is anything broken?"

"I don't think so," I said. "But I can't get up."

She started to poke around my back, and I lay there and groaned.

"Carlos, we'll need the stretcher," she said to a man standing outside the fort. Then she touched my cheek. "Did you walk here by yourself?" she asked.

"I rode my bike," I said. "It's in the trees."

The man came back and the two of them lifted me onto the stretcher. I screamed when they picked me up, it hurt so bad—not just my back, but my neck too. Then they strapped me onto the stretcher, and the pain got a little better. It was a weird feeling when they picked up the stretcher. All of a sudden I was floating in the air without moving a muscle.

Then we were outside the fort and I was being carried through the trees toward the red flashing lights. I could see Jujube standing nearby, her face all sucked in. Rick was next to her.

"Hi, Sophie," he said.

I was so embarrassed I looked away. He must have thought I was such a loser.

I don't understand what happened next. Maybe I was tired, or maybe all that pain mixed up my brain. But suddenly I got this weird feeling that Jujube was right. The aliens had come, like she'd said they would. And they were carrying me toward a spaceship with red and white flashing lights.

Then everything faded out like the end of a movie, and there was just darkness.

Chapter Nine

When I woke, I was lying flat on my back in a small room. The bed had steel rails around it, and there was a TV over my head. I could see another girl lying in a bed on the other side of the room. She was watching the TV above her head.

I was in a hospital. And it was the middle of the day. I could tell because sunlight was pushing through the window as if nothing could keep it out. It was giving me a headache.

"Well, it's good to see you open your eyes, kiddo," said a voice.

I tried to turn my head to see who was talking, but I couldn't. Something was holding my neck in place. And I could feel something else, down between my legs. It hurt. Then I realized it was the tube for a pee bag. I couldn't move. I couldn't even pee on my own. What was wrong with me?

"Don't try to move your head," said the voice. "We've got a brace on you."

A nurse's head showed up where I could see it—right over my face. She smiled down at me and straightened my blankets.

"Why can't I move?" I whispered. My heart was pounding—I mean *really* pounding.

"Don't worry," said the nurse. "You're going to be all right. Your neck and back need complete rest so they can heal. We want you to rest in this brace for a few days. Then you'll be fine, just like before."

"Oh." I almost started crying, I was so

relieved. For a minute I'd thought I was going to be in a wheelchair.

"Now that you're awake, I can go tell your friend," said the nurse. "She seems to have moved into our waiting room for good. Won't go to school or anything."

With another smile, the nurse left the room. Then I heard running footsteps, and a different face poked itself over mine. When I saw Jujube, a grin took over my whole face.

"Oh, Froggy," she whispered. "I'm so glad you're not dead!"

"Thanks, I guess," I said.

Something splashed onto my face and I realized Jujube was crying. "Well," she mumbled, "when your eyes closed like that…"

I didn't want to think about it, so I tried to joke her out of it. "When they stuck me in the ambulance, I got the weirdest feeling," I said. "As if it was a spaceship, and your aliens were finally taking me to outer space."

Jujube didn't even smile. "Froggy," she said, "your mom and dad are here. They went to get something to eat. I think your dad's kind of mad. Ms. Lee said they can't see you unless she's here too."

I just stared at her. My dad? What was I going to say to him? And why wouldn't Ms. Lee let him see me? "What am I going to do?" I whispered.

"I dunno," Jujube said. "Maybe you should tell somebody what happened. Like…maybe Ms. Lee? She seems nice."

"I can't," I said. What was Jujube thinking? I couldn't go blabbing things to Ms. Lee. If I did, my dad might hurt my mom to get back at me.

Jujube leaned over me and stared right into my face. Her green eye was very green. "Why can't you?" she asked.

I closed my eyes. I was so scared, all I could think about was how hard my heart was pounding. Then the nurse came back into the room. She hooked a tray over the steel rails on my bed and said, "Time for lunch, kiddo. Someone's going to have to feed you."

I stared at her. Someone had to feed me? Why? Then I remembered the brace on my back.

The nurse grinned at me. "You're just going to have to lie there like a baby. Nothing to do but open wide."

"Let me do it," Jujube said. "Let me feed her."

The nurse smiled at me and asked, "Should I trust this kid with your life?"

My life but not my lunch, I thought.

"This is service," said Jujube, picking up the spoon. The nurse laughed and left the room.

"Open wide," said Jujube. "This is the most awesome-looking muck I've ever seen."

What choice did I have? I opened my mouth. Jujube fed me the food, bite by bite. It was peas and carrots, potatoes and meat. She wouldn't tell me what it was, so I had to guess by tasting. But I wasn't really thinking about what I was eating. I was trying to think up something to tell Ms. Lee. She wouldn't believe me if I said I fell out of my bedroom window. I would need broken bones for a story like that.

I thought, chewed and swallowed. Jujube started shoving the food into my mouth faster and faster. It was hard to keep up.

"Hey," I said. "Slow down. I'll choke to death."

"Not funny," said Jujube. She sniffed, and I realized she was crying again. "I wish they'd come, those aliens," she said. "But I don't think they're real anymore. I just don't think so."

I didn't say anything. *Welcome to real life*, I thought.

"Hello, Sophie," said a voice from the doorway. Right away my heart started pounding again. I didn't have to see this person to know who she was—trouble with a capital T. *Ms. Lee.*

"Hi," I said and stared at the ceiling.

"Jujube," she said, "I want you to leave the room. I need to talk to Sophie alone."

I couldn't see Jujube as she walked out, but I could guess what she was doing—crying her eyes out. I hated Ms. Lee for sending her away.

"How are you, Sophie?" Ms. Lee came over and stood by my bed where I could see her.

What a stupid question, I thought. *Stupid question, stupid answer.*

"Fine," I said.

"The doctor tells me they should be able to remove the brace in a few days," she said.

"That's good," I said. "Then I can go back to school."

Make it look good, I thought.

"Yes," said Ms. Lee. "We need to talk about that and a few other things."

"What other things?" I asked quickly. I could hear it in her voice—trouble was coming. But maybe I could talk my way out of it. This time the problem was just my back and some bruises—not something important like stealing.

"Sophie, what happened to you?" asked Ms. Lee.

I lay there, just thinking and thinking. I could say a car hit me. That would explain the bruises and my sore back and neck. But there would have been cuts and scrapes too. No matter how hard I thought, I couldn't think of anything that made sense. I decided to keep my mouth shut and say nothing. I just lay there and stared at her.

Ms. Lee sighed. "Sophie," she said, "I don't know how to help you. You're going to have to tell me sooner or later. The life you're living right now isn't safe for you."

I couldn't turn my head to get her out of my face, so I closed my eyes. But she kept talking.

"Your mother and father are out in the hall," she said quietly. "Because I don't know what happened, they're not allowed to be alone with you. I'm going to let them into the room now, but remember—I'll be here the whole time. I want to be sure you're safe."

I heard her walk away. Even though I didn't say so, I was glad she wasn't going to leave me alone with my dad. I didn't think he'd do anything in the hospital, but I still didn't want to be alone with him.

Footsteps came into the room. Slowly I opened my eyes. My parents were leaning over me. My mom's eyes were red. My dad's were black.

I felt it happen then, the way it always did around my dad. All the power went out of me—the power to figure out things, to talk. It disappeared, and all that was left was a dead, empty space inside me. My dad always made me feel like that—as if I couldn't do anything. There was no point in even trying.

My dad was hanging onto his shirt collar with one hand. One finger was pressed across his throat. It was such a little thing, Ms. Lee wouldn't notice it. Even if she did, she wouldn't know what it meant. But I did. It meant, *You're dead meat if you tell.*

My dad didn't have to worry. I wasn't talking.

My mom stood next to him, twisting her hands around the bed railing. I knew what she was thinking. If I messed up and talked, she would get it too.

"Hello, Froggy," said my dad. Then, right in front of Ms. Lee, he leaned down and kissed my forehead. My stomach just about exploded then—a nuclear bomb inside.

"Are you all right, hon?" my mom whispered. She looked so white.

"Yeah," I said. "Are you?"

Before my mom could answer, my dad said, "We've been so worried about you. What happened?"

I looked at the finger on his neck and closed my eyes. "I can't remember," I said. It was all I could think of, but it made me feel better. Nobody could get mad at me for this.

My dad sounded happy with my answer. "It was that boyfriend of yours, I bet," he said. "It's okay, hon. You can tell us."

I realized he was giving me an answer— one that was okay with him. But I didn't want to get Larry into trouble. He'd dumped me, but he hadn't beaten me up.

"I don't know," I said, keeping my eyes closed. "I can't remember."

Ms. Lee started talking again. She sounded cold and hard, almost like a machine. "Well, Sophie, I want you to try to remember."

I got really mad at her then. Didn't she realize that my mom and dad and I had a system all worked out? My dad brought home the money, and my mom and I kept his secrets. He was the boss, and we did what he said. As long as we all followed his system, everything worked out fine. It was when a social worker showed up at our house that we got into trouble.

"Sophie," said Ms. Lee, "I want you to open your eyes."

Beth Goobie

You've got to be kidding, I thought. I kept my eyes shut tight. For a moment there was complete silence, and then a new voice started talking. It wasn't next to my bed but farther away, by the door.

"She's scared," said Jujube. "That's why she can't tell you."

My eyes flew open and I saw Jujube standing behind Ms. Lee. Her green eye was greener than I'd ever seen it. It flashed like an ambulance light, like a spaceship light. Jujube from outer space.

"Shut up, will you?" I hissed.

Jujube looked straight at Ms. Lee. She said, "I'm going to tell because I'm more scared than she is. I'm scared she'll be dead one of these days. It's her dad, Ms. Lee. It's her dad who hits her."

76

Chapter Ten

The silence seemed to go on forever. Every-one froze and stared at Jujube. Because she'd gone and done the impossible—she'd just *said* it.

Then things started to move again. My mom stepped back from the bed. I knew she was trying to get out of my dad's reach, so he couldn't hit her. I wished I was her. I couldn't move because of my brace, and he was right beside my head. I thought, *This is it*, and closed my eyes.

I forgot, of course, that my dad was a great actor. He never yelled or swore in front of other people. I heard him take a big breath, probably to get his voice ready so it would sound real. Then he started talking as if he was discussing the weather.

"Now now now, Jujube," he said. "Where did you get that idea?"

Jujube stepped forward so she was standing next to Ms. Lee. Then she glared straight at my dad. I didn't see how she could do that. My dad's face was the last place I was going to look.

"I've seen the bruises you put on her," Jujube said. "I saw the bump on her head. You hit her so hard she goes black and blue." Her voice wobbled. Ms. Lee put an arm around her.

My dad said, "I'm very concerned about the bruises Froggy's been coming home with." He sounded worried, just like a TV dad. "It must be that new boyfriend. What's his name, sweetie? Larry, isn't it?"

I just lay there with my eyes closed. No way, *no way*, NO WAY was I saying anything.

"Why didn't you report these incidents to the police?" asked Ms. Lee. She sounded mad.

"I was keeping track of them," said my dad. He put out his hand and patted my head. His finger touched a scab from a beer bottle he'd hit me with last week. Quickly he moved his hand to my forehead.

His hand felt heavier than I can tell you. I kept my eyes closed and shut everything out. "I don't remember," I said. "That happens sometimes, y'know. I just don't remember."

I had seen TV shows where people got hurt and then forgot what happened. I figured if it worked on TV, it could work for me too. All of a sudden I wished I was watching this on TV so I could change the channel to another show.

"Why don't we give Sophie a break?" said Ms. Lee. For the first time, I liked the lady. Finally she was showing some common sense. "We can discuss this at a later time," she said. "I'm asking you to leave the room now, Mr. Hawthorne."

For a second my dad's hand tightened across my forehead. I got the message, but I don't think Ms. Lee noticed. Then my dad bent down and kissed my cheek. I could feel his breath on my face. I kept my eyes closed so I didn't have to see him.

"I'll be waiting in the car, hon," he said to my mom. Then he walked out of the room.

I opened my eyes to see Jujube standing next to me. She looked relieved that my dad was gone. "Can I stay?" she asked.

Ms. Lee was about to answer when my mom spoke up. It sounded as if she was over by the window. "May I talk to my daughter alone?" she asked.

Ms. Lee looked at me carefully. Then she

said, "I'm sorry, Mrs. Hawthorne. I'll have to stay here with you."

She sent Jujube out of the room and waited while my mom came over to my bed. At first I couldn't look at my mom, my heart was pounding too hard. Then all I could do was stare at her. I mean, this was my mom standing beside me. She could get hurt because of what Jujube had said. And it was all my fault. *Stupid, no good, nothing girl.*

My mom stood for a long time without saying anything. She just stared at her hands and twisted her purse strap around. Then she started crying.

"I didn't know, Froggy," she whispered. "I didn't know he would go this far. This is my fault. I should've done something. I should've gotten you out of there a long time ago."

"No, Mom," I said. "It's not your fault, it's mine."

My mom stared at me. "But I'm your mother. I'm the one who let this happen to you."

I stared back at her. She wasn't making sense. How could it be her fault? I was the one who got beat up. If I hadn't gotten beat up, there wouldn't have been any trouble.

"Do you really feel this is your fault, Sophie?" Ms. Lee asked softly.

"It's got to be," I said. Suddenly I was crying in big ugly sobs. "My dad only hits me when I do something wrong," I said. "He only hits me because I'm bad. I'm bad and he's trying to make me good. Maybe when I'm good, then he can love me. But I don't know how to be good. How can I be good and make my dad love me? I just want my dad to love me. But he can't. He can't because I'm stupid. I'm a stupid, no good, nothing girl."

Silence filled the room. But the words weren't finished coming out of me yet. "If my dad loved me," I said, still crying, "then I would be something. Then I could be something."

"Oh, Sophie," my mom whispered. "You are something. You're some*one*."

Then she leaned down and held me for a long time. Around us the room got very quiet. I think the girl across the room turned off her TV. My mom was crying. I was crying. I think even Ms. Lee was crying.

Finally my mom stood up again. But she took my hand and held it.

Ms. Lee smiled at me. She took my other hand. "When your father hits you, it's his fault," she said. "Not yours. *His*."

For a minute my mind shut down. It just stopped working, as if it had hit a brick wall. *No*, I thought. *It isn't my dad's fault. It can't be. He doesn't really want to hit me. He's just doing it to straighten me out.*

Did my dad *want* to hurt me?

"No," I said and closed my eyes.

It got very quiet again. Then my mom touched my cheek and said, "Maybe it's time you and I said it's your dad's fault, Sophie."

My mom had never called me "Sophie" before. Only social workers and teachers and kids at school called me that. But it sounded like me for the first time when I heard it come out of my mom's mouth.

After this, Ms. Lee and my mom talked for a long time. They talked about filing a police report. Ms. Lee said something about a "restraining order." The longer they talked, the more I felt something happening inside me. It was as if some kind of space was growing there, but it wasn't outer space. It was space inside me for something besides fear—fear and running and trying to figure out how to not get hit. Because my mom was doing that now, with Ms. Lee. They were figuring that out so I didn't have to.

And neither did Jujube. I could just see her in the doorway, peeking into the room. For the first time in years, she didn't look worried. Our eyes met and I grinned at her—a little grin, but it counted.

She came over to my bed. "You're not mad at me, are you, Froggy?" she asked.

"No," I smiled and took her hand.

Chapter Eleven

Ms. Lee took my mom to a women's shelter. Over the next few days, they both visited me. The police came and helped me fill out a report about the assault. Jujube visited in the evenings because she wasn't allowed to skip any more classes. She was mad about this, but I told her school was good for her. She had her future to think about.

My mom told me about the shelter. She said the windows were made of bulletproof glass, and the doors had huge locks and chains on them. She said the place was full of women and children, and she had a lot of people to talk to. It surprised her that there were so many other women with the same problem.

For the first time in my life, I stopped worrying about my mom. I didn't even have to worry about myself. The hospital wouldn't let my dad come near me. My mom had a restraining order from the police, which meant he couldn't come near either of us. He couldn't even call us on the phone. At first I was surprised people believed what my mom and I said about my dad. He was such a good talker, everyone had always believed him. But Ms. Lee and the police and the hospital just took over and kept my dad away.

The police showed me some pictures they'd taken the night the ambulance brought me to the hospital. I was still out of it then, so I didn't know about them. When I saw the bruises in the pictures, it made me think of my dad. I felt as if he was standing right beside me, staring at me with his black eyes.

One of the cops smiled at me. "Your father has been charged, Sophie. The restraining order means he has to stay away from you and your mother. The trial will be in a few months."

For a minute I felt dumb. The cop could tell I was scared, just like a little kid. She must have thought I was stupid. *Stupid, no good, nothing girl.*

But the cop didn't look as if she thought I was stupid. She smiled as if she liked me, and then she went on talking. She said they wanted me to be a witness at the trial. Ms. Lee and a lawyer would help me get ready for it.

At night, when I was alone, I had nightmares about my dad and woke up crying. But during the day I stopped feeling as if he was waiting around every corner. I think my mom felt safer too. She stood straighter when she came to visit. She didn't look at the ground as much, and sometimes she even smiled.

After a few days, the doctors took the brace off my back. I could sit up and feed myself. This was a relief, because Jujube had started to play games when she fed me. She would say, "The aliens told me to give you this message." Then she would dribble gravy on my face and start laughing. Sometimes she could be such a pain, but then, she was only twelve.

The day after I got my brace off, Ms. Lee walked into my room with my mom. They brought chairs over to my bed. I could see this meant a long talk, and I started to get nervous. I remembered Ms. Lee saying, "We need to talk about that and a few other things."

What other things?

Ms. Lee and my mom looked at each other. Then Ms. Lee said, "Sophie, your mother has been hurt quite badly by your father. Not only in her body. Your father also hurt your mother in the way she thinks and feels about life. This takes a long time to heal."

I looked back and forth between them, wondering what was coming next. My mom didn't look at me. She stared out the window, like old times. All of a sudden I got a crazy thought. I thought, *She's going back to my dad. We're moving back with my dad.*

But then my mom looked at me. She had so much love and worry in her eyes, and it was all for me. I knew it wouldn't happen then—she wouldn't go back to my dad.

My mom took my hand and said, "Sophie, this is just for a while—about four months or so. I'm going into a treatment program for people who have problems…drinking problems. It's here in Edmonton, so I can call and visit you a lot. And I'm going back to school so I can get a better job. Then I can support the two of us."

My head was spinning and spinning. I couldn't figure out what she was saying. She was going into a treatment program for drinking? Was I going into the program with her? But she hadn't said anything about me.

Did that mean I was going somewhere else? But where? Back to my dad? *Was I going back to my dad?*

"Sophie," my mom said, "you're going to live in a group home for a while. Not forever—just four months, until I get things together."

I stared at her. A group home? She was sending me to live in a group home? But I didn't know anyone there. It would be full of freaks and weirdos. They might be worse than my dad. And no one would want to be friends with me if I lived in a group home.

"You'll get help at the group home too, Sophie," Ms. Lee said.

I got so mad at her then, I wanted to slug her. I wished she would just shut her mouth. She was the one who put this idea into my mom's head, I was sure of it. My mom and I were okay by ourselves. We didn't need anyone's help.

But Ms. Lee just kept on talking. "Your mother hasn't been able to give you the time or the help she wants to, Sophie," she said. "You need time to figure out how you feel about things. The group home staff will be able to help you with that."

I figured this was an insult. "You're saying I've got problems?" I asked.

Ms. Lee looked me straight in the eye. "You have things to work out," she said. "You're still on probation, and you'll continue to visit me every two weeks. You're behind in school and you need extra help there. And the group home staff can help you when you go to court."

"I don't need help," I muttered.

Ms. Lee shook her head. "Living in a group home can be fun, Sophie. You go swimming and camping. There are other kids living there that you can get to know."

"They're probably all nutcases," I said.

Ms. Lee looked a little angry. "They're just kids like you," she said.

This didn't make me feel any better. "I want to live with my mom," I said. I stared at her, trying to make her change her mind just by looking at her.

But it didn't work. My mom just turned her head and stared out the window. "You will live with me, Sophie," she said. "In a while. Four months isn't so long, is it?"

She started to cry. Well, that did it. I didn't want to cause her any trouble, so I shut up. It didn't matter what I thought anyway. It was all decided.

After they left, I lay in my bed and stared out the window. It felt like the end of the world, as if everything important had just gotten up and walked away from me. First, I'd been dumb enough to get beat up, so I'd lost my dad. And now I was losing my mom. All that was left was me—a stupid, no good, nothing girl.

That night, Jujube brought Rick to visit. At first I didn't know where to look. There I was, sitting in my bed in a dumb hospital gown. I'd been crying, so my eyes were red, and I didn't have any makeup on. I must have looked gross.

Jujube sat on the side of my bed and looked back and forth between Rick and me. She grinned like a cat when I told them about the group home.

"I'll phone you every day," she said. "I'll come visit you."

"You're not worried about the weirdos I'll be living with?" I asked. Then I remembered Rick had a friend who was living in a group home. He would probably hate me for saying something like that. I stared down at my hands, hoping he wouldn't get mad.

He didn't sound mad. He just said, "You're going to a group home because your dad beat you, not because you're killing people in shopping malls."

"I guess," I said.

"Hey," he said. "Maybe you'll end up at the same one Bert's living in."

This made me kind of laugh. I looked at him quickly and he grinned at me. "Then I could visit you both at the same time," he said.

This really made me laugh. I was kind of nervous, but Rick and Jujube laughed too, so I didn't feel too stupid. Suddenly words started coming out of me again—the truth, like it had with Ms. Lee and my mom.

"I guess I think maybe my mom's going crazy," I said. I started to cry again. Here I'd just been laughing, and a minute later I was crying. But I couldn't help it. "It's because of everything that's happened," I said. "It's making my mom go crazy, but she won't tell me. Ms. Lee won't tell me either."

There was a moment of silence, so quiet it almost hurt. Then Jujube said, "So what if she is for a while? She's trying to get better, isn't she? Just give her a chance."

"I guess," I said, staring at my hands. "But I'm scared. What if she really goes off the deep end? Then I'd have to go live with my dad."

"No way!" said Jujube, jumping up. "Never ever EVER!" Her green eye was really green.

"That wouldn't happen," said Rick. "Just ask Ms. Lee. She'll tell you."

"I guess," I said again. "But it's more than my mom. Nothing's the same now. Everything's different. And I've got to go live in a group home with people I don't know. It feels like I'm moving to outer space. I didn't want any of this to happen. I wanted my dad to stop hitting me, but I didn't want the rest of it."

For a long minute, Jujube and Rick just looked at me. Then Jujube said, "Not everything is different. I'm not different, and I'm still your friend. I'll come visit you no matter where you live. So will your mom, Froggy. You'll see."

"Not Froggy," Rick told her quietly. "Her name's Sophie." He looked at me and said, "I'll visit you too, Sophie."

I started to go red and looked away. *No you won't*, I thought. But I didn't say it.

"I guess," I said. "I just wish things were okay with my dad and none of this had happened."

"But it *did* happen," Jujube said loudly. "And now things have to change so it won't happen again."

When she said this, a bright clear feeling went through me and I understood what she meant. Because she was right. Something *had* happened that had changed things for good. There was no point in wishing it hadn't happened, or trying to cover it up. But I still had my mom and Jujube, and I still had me. Me—the stupid, no good, nothing girl.

No, I thought. *The something girl. SomeONE.*

I took a deep breath. *Okay,* I thought. *I'm someone, and I'm moving to a group home. Not to outer space, and not to the end of the earth. It's just a home with other kids like me.*

I looked at Jujube and smiled—a little smile, but it counted.

"I guess," I said.

Chapter Twelve

Ms. Lee's car pulled up to the curb and parked. I looked out the window at the group home. It didn't look weird. There was a garage and a tree, and a teenage girl sitting on the front steps. Not exactly outer space, I guess.

We got out of the car and walked up to the house. Ms. Lee was on one side of me, my mom on the other.

"Hi," said the girl on the steps. "You the new girl?"

"I guess," I said.

"Awesome," she said. "I'm Helen." She grinned, then got up and opened the front door. "I'll tell staff you're here."

We followed her into the house. Inside, there was noise coming from everywhere. A stereo was playing, girls were talking, and I could hear someone running down some stairs. This was completely different from my house. For a second I got scared and looked at my mom. She looked nervous too.

But then I thought, *No more having to be quiet all the time. Quiet and hiding and listening for my dad's footsteps so I know where he is.* When I thought this, I felt a soft peace fill me, even in the middle of all that noise.

Helen stuck her head out of a doorway down the hall. "This way," she called. "The office is in here."

We went into the office and met a staff named Rick. *Rick*, I thought. *I like that name.* This cheered me up, even if it wasn't the Rick I wanted. We sat in the office, and Rick explained the group home rules. Then he showed me around the house. I met the other girls and another staff named Brenda, who was cooking supper.

Then Ms. Lee and my mom had to go. I walked them to the car and watched as they got in. My mom rolled down her window and looked at me. She tried to smile.

"It seems nice," she said. "You'll be all right here, hon. I promise I'll visit and call a lot."

I tried to smile back. "Yeah," I said. "You'd better. Or I might forget all about you."

I was trying to make a joke, and I think my mom could tell. She reached out the window and took my hand. "No you won't," she said. "Promise?"

I smiled—a little one, but it counted. "All right," I said. "I promise to call you too."

I watched them drive away, then went back to the house. Helen was waiting on the steps and we talked for a while. She'd lived in the group home for three months, so she knew how to explain things. While I listened, I thought, *She seems pretty normal*. Maybe a bit tough—she had a couple of tattoos, but she wasn't a freak or a weirdo.

After talking to Helen, I went to my new bedroom and unpacked the clothes Ms. Lee had bought me. Then I sat on my bed and listened to the noise going on in the rest of the house. How was I ever going to get used to it—all that laughing and talking, and the stereo playing so loud? When Helen called me for supper, I just sat and watched the other girls joke with staff. There were five girls and two staff, so there was a lot of talking. Then we all had to do chores. I helped Helen with the dishes. This was when I noticed the chore chart on the kitchen wall. My name was already on it, every day of the week.

"Just like home, eh?" Helen said.

"I guess," I said.

After supper we watched a video, and then I went to my room and finished unpacking. Soon it was time for lights out. I lay in the dark, listening to the house go quiet. Everything felt strange. I was lying in a strange bed in a strange darkness. Because I couldn't see anything, it felt like I was in the middle of nowhere. Without my mom and dad I was nowhere, nobody, nothing.

No, I thought. *I'm the something girl. THE SOMETHING GIRL.*

But I was still lonely, and this made me think about my mom. What kind of bed was she lying in? Did the darkness feel strange to her? Then, for a second, I wondered about my dad. Was he feeling lonely? Was he sad? Was he sorry for what he'd done to me? Did he wish he could change it?

For a second I wished I could change it. For one sad, hurting moment, I wished with everything I was that I could change it.

But then I remembered it was my dad who'd done the beating up, not me. So he had to change it. He had to change himself.

A soft peace came into me again and I fell asleep. In the morning I woke up and looked around, totally clued out. I didn't know where I was. Then I heard a knock, and Brenda poked her head through the door.

"Time to get up," she said. "You've got school today."

I got dressed and went out into the hall. Then I waited until I saw Helen come out of her room. I followed her around and copied everything she did. When she went to the kitchen, I walked in after her. When she poured herself some Shreddies, so did I. I even put on three teaspoons of sugar, like she did, and drank some orange juice. Then I followed her to the washroom and brushed my teeth next to her.

"Hey," she grinned at me. "I've got a twin."

I went really red and ducked my head. "Sorry," I said.

Helen just laughed. "No prob," she said. "I've always wanted a twin."

By 8:20, the other girls had left for school. Brenda said she would give me a ride, so I sat in the living room and waited. It was getting late, but I didn't want to complain. Then I heard a car horn honk outside.

Brenda came into the living room and smiled at me. "Why don't you see who that is?" she asked.

I opened the front door and looked out. An old blue Ford was parked by the curb. Beside it stood Rick, grinning at me. Jujube was on the car roof, waving madly.

"Sophie," she yelled. "C'mon, it's the aliens. We've landed and we're going to take you to outer space."

She had a blue-and-green triangle pinned to her shirt. Rick was wearing one too. When I got to the car, Jujube handed me a third triangle and a safety pin, and I pinned it to my shirt.

"See?" Jujube grinned. "It did come true. Just like I said."

"Yup," I grinned at her. "Just like you said."

Brenda handed me a bag lunch and I got into the front seat beside Rick. Jujube sat behind us, blabbing away. This was fine with me because I didn't have a clue what to say.

I mean, Rick was *gorgeous*. He was just *so gorgeous*. For a second I wished Helen and the other girls could see me sitting beside him.

"Why don't I drive you to school for the rest of the year?" asked Rick. "It's only three more weeks and not that far out of my way."

"Sure!" I said.

"All right then," he grinned. "That's settled. Now, where would you like to go—Venus or Mars?"

"Pluto," I grinned back. "As long as we make it to school by nine. Or Ms. Lee will get on my case."

"School it is, then," said Rick. "Pluto will have to wait for another day." He started the car and we drove down the street.

OTHER TITLES IN THE ORCA SOUNDINGS SERIES